Chapter 1

BEN WAS often at Clare's house. He was there when she was talking about her birthday. She wasn't having a party, but her mother said, "For a treat, we'd like to take you to the theatre to see 'Cinderella', if you'd like that."

"Yes, *please*," said Clare. 'Cinderella' was a favourite story.

Her mother said, "I'll book tickets, then."

"And a ticket for Ben?" said Clare.

"And a ticket for Ben," said her mother. "And we'll bring Ben back to a late tea – well, supper really."

"Birthday *supper*," said Ben. "Will there be candles, if it's supper?"

And Clare's mother said of course there would be candles on the cake.

Ben hadn't been to the theatre before, and he enjoyed everything about it – the seat that tipped up, clusters of lights above, and gold painting on the ceiling. Then the lights dimmed, the play began, and Ben thought about nothing else at all.

Afterwards, in the dark, the street was hung with Christmas lights, almost as though 'Cinderella' was still going on. And then there was supper.

His baby brother was in bed when Ben got home. That, and going to the theatre, made him feel very grown up.

When his birthday was coming, he said to his mother, "Can we go to 'Cinderella' for my birthday?"

But 'Cinderella' wasn't at the theatre now. It had finished long ago. He looked so disappointed, his mother said, "It must have been really special."

3

"Better than a party," said Ben.

What else could be better than a party? his mother wondered. Later in the day she thought of something he had enjoyed enormously once before.

"Ben," she said, "for your birthday treat, would you like to go to the zoo?"

"Oh, yes!" said Ben.

"Good idea," said his father. "We'll all go. Maybe Daniel will fall asleep in the push-chair when he's tired."

Ben hoped so. They were always coming away early from things because Daniel got tired, and then was cross.

"You can take a friend," said his mother. "One friend."

"Clare," said Ben.

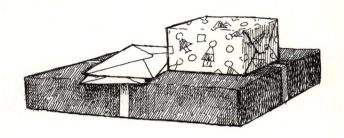

Chapter 2

WHEN THE day came, it started well with the postman bringing four cards and two presents.

Then the telephone rang, and somebody was ill, he could tell. His mother was being asked to look after someone. Who was it?

His mother was saying, "We'll pick him up. Don't worry. The picnic's all ready, and we're leaving in a few minutes."

5

It was only morning! Not long after breakfast. Were they going already? She came back and said, "Ben, James's mother has a high temperature. I've said we'll take him with us."

"Not to the zoo!" Ben nearly shouted. "Not James!"

Anybody else would have been better. He never liked James much. They often fought and squabbled, but their mothers were friends. His mother said, "You have to learn to get on with lots of people, not just special friends."

"Not on my birthday!" said Ben.

"Specially not James."

But it was no use. His mother said, "There's plenty of space at the zoo. And James likes Daniel. I dare say he'll push him along. Sorry, Ben."

It was true that James was nice to Daniel. He hadn't a little brother or sister. And Clare was coming. Perhaps he wouldn't have to bother with James much. Then he remembered something, and said, "I didn't know we were going so early. It's only morning."

His mother looked at his father, and he thought his father shook his head.

"Why did you shake your head?" said Ben.

His father said, "I've got a tickle in my ear."

Ben didn't think he had. His eyes were smiling, as if he had a secret, but he only said, "We must get on." He

8

picked up his camera, and got busy packing the picnic and then Daniel into the car.

Soon they were at Clare's house, and she was waiting at the gate, with a present. It was a mouth organ, but Ben had to put it in his pocket. He wasn't allowed to blow it in the car.

James was ready and waiting too. He climbed into the car, saying, "Happy Birthday, Ben," and pushing a present into Ben's hand.

"Thank you," said Ben. "Oh, good, it's a police car. Blue glass."

9

Perhaps it was going to be all right, having James with them. And it was, on the journey, and at first at the zoo. But Ben and Clare wanted to stop at each cage, and stand and stare and talk about the animals. James wanted to go rushing on to the next thing.

But even James stood and watched the orang-utan with her baby. They all

did, Daniel too. She sat and cradled it in her arms, just as a human mother did. She held its head tenderly against her mouth, then turned the baby's face to hers.

"She kissed it," said Clare. "She did, Ben. Did you see?"

The mother now turned the baby's head away from the visitors, but it wanted to see them and kept twisting round. Ben's father took a photograph.

In the aquarium James was a nuisance. He banged on the glass with his hand, and a terrified catfish darted away.

"James!" said Ben's father. "Don't do that any more!"

Clare said, "I was just looking at its eye."

James said, "It was a dopey fish, not doing anything."

Ben said, "How'd you like a stupid giant thumping at your window?"

"Stupid giant yourself!" shouted James.

And they started to push each other around. Daniel began to cry. It was an awful sound down there in the half dark of the aquarium.

"Everybody out!" said Ben's father, apologising to the nearest people.

"We haven't finished looking," said Ben, but his father said they were fighting, not looking.

After that there was peace for a while as they watched the pelicans and the flamingoes.

Chapter 3

TROUBLE BEGAN again outside the Ape House, where there was a statue – the head of a famous gorilla, dead now. James got to it first and pointed, pulling a face, and shouting, "He was called Alfred. Isn't he horrible! Isn't he ugly and beastly!"

Before anyone else could speak, a lady said, "He was not horrible. You didn't know Alfred. I did, and he was my friend."

15

A gorilla for a friend. They all waited in silence for her to go on.

"When I was a little girl, I walked down that path there, holding his hand, and we sat on a seat together. As he grew older, and boys like you behaved badly to him and mocked him through the bars, he did get cross. I'm not surprised."

"Nor am I," said Ben's mother.

His father looked at his watch and said he was sorry but they must go now. Ben was shocked. He thought he meant

go home, finish the visit to the zoo. He hadn't even seen the giraffes and he specially wanted to see them.

But it was all right. They followed a sign to the door of the Giraffe House, and pushed it open. It swung to behind them. In the dim light, three giraffes towered above them, looking even taller indoors. One was drinking from a dish that was fixed on the railings.

Clare said, "She's slopping a bit, but the dish is shallow, that's why."

They were reading the notice about the young giraffe when something happened. James and Ben found themselves *covered* with hay. It was all over their heads and shoulders.

They spun round and found two elephants looking at them. The big-eared one was just drawing her trunk back.

"*It* did that," said James.

Ben said, "I didn't hear them *or* see them."

And Clare hadn't, either.

Ben's father said, "That elephant's annoyed with us. We all turned our backs and gazed up at the giraffes. She's jealous."

"An elephant jealous?" said Ben.

"Like you," said his mother, "if visitors take too much notice of Daniel."

"Not like me," said Ben, but he knew it was. His father was gathering up the hay, meaning to hand it back, but the same elephant blew hard down her trunk, and a spray of water came out.

"Ugh!" said Clare, and Ben said, "It's *spitting* at us."

James stepped forward to the barrier, flapping his glove, and saying, "You cheeky thing!"

But the elephant's trunk shot out and grabbed the glove.

"Hey! Give it back!" said James.

But Clare said, "It was your own fault."

Ben asked, "Will the keeper get it back?" But his father said if he did it would look as though he was on James's side, when James had been annoying the elephant. Keepers had to work with animals every day whether they were ill or well, happy or bad-tempered.

Ben's mother said, "Who'd want to be in a cage with an angry elephant?"

James looked really bothered now. His gloves were nearly new.

It was only then they saw a sign. It was in capitals, but it was right at the back of the cage, and it said:

BEWARE
OF THESE ANIMALS
TAKING YOUR HANDBAGS, ETC.

They now read the names of the elephants too – Wendy, the Indian elephant, Christina, the African, with the larger ears. It was Christina who had thrown the hay, and snatched the glove.

Doors at the far end were opened and fastened back. A keeper came forward, saying, "Ah, who's the one with the birthday, then?"

Ben just looked at him. How did *he* know?

Clare smiled and said, "It's Ben."

"Right," said the keeper. "Happy birthday, Ben." To the elephants he said, "Now Wendy and Christina, I'd like really good behaviour from you two. This is a great day for Ben, and he's come to share something with you."

Have I? thought Ben. What? The picnic wouldn't last long with two elephants. Besides, there were notices about NOT feeding the animals.

What he didn't know was that his mother had telephoned about the birthday visit. She had asked if they might

bring the elephants an apple and a banana each. And permission had been given.

James thought the keeper was going to give them the fruit, so he said, "Make Christina give my glove back first."

But the keeper said that was bribing, and he didn't bribe his animals.

"If I said, 'Be good and I'll give you something special', they'd expect it all the time. They'd try to insist on it, and then where would I be? I work here every day."

He drew Ben to the left of him, opposite Wendy. He drew James to his right, opposite Christina. Ben's mother gave an apple to each boy. Only then did Ben realise that they would be

doing the feeding.

Christina's trunk twitched, then stretched out in front of James, two big damp grey nostrils. James was nervous and drew back.

"No teasing," said the keeper. "Hold your arm out."

Christina took the apple neatly, and James was pleased. Wendy had already taken Ben's, and he was beaming. She had swung her trunk under to place the apple far back in her mouth.

"Now the young lady's turn," said the keeper. "Give this banana to Wendy. And, Ben, give this one to Christina."

By now everybody was happy, visitors and elephants. But that wasn't the end. What Ben and Clare and James had not known was that this was the elephants' bath morning.

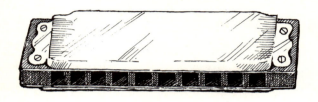

Chapter 4

IN WARM weather there was water outside for the elephants to splash in. In
cold weather they had their baths
inside. The floor was cleaned, and the
keeper's assistant had the hosepipe and
brushes ready. First, he threw the glove
over to James, then he turned on the
tap. Water gushed out of the hosepipe,
and the keeper tested it to make sure it
was nice and warm.

"Like you for Daniel, Mum," said Ben.

The keeper began to spray Christina, and the assistant scrubbed her with a long-handled brush, even behind her ears. The visitors could see that she was enjoying it all. Sometimes she held her mouth opposite the end of the hose. They could see her tongue – very pale pink, and thick and short.

Wendy played a trick on the keeper. She placed her foot on the hosepipe. The water stopped, and she looked at the visitors who laughed out loud. The keeper said, "Wendy, leave it!" And she did, but James said she smiled.

The keeper moved to the side of Christina, and touched her near foot with his boot. Quietly, he said, "Christina, lift it." And she did. He washed the underneath part of that foot, and

31

moved to the next and the next and the next. Each time, he said, "Lift it", and she did. No trouble at all.

James said, "She does just as he tells her, Ben."

Ben said, "He didn't even have to tell her twice."

"That's one done," said the keeper, and the tap was turned off. He chained Christina by a back leg. Wendy would have her bath now without Christina pushing in and trying to share it.

Then came the next surprise for Ben. The keeper came to him and said, "It's your turn now." Ben backed away. Turn for what? He didn't fancy a bath from a hosepipe today. But the keeper said, "For an extra birthday treat, you can help to bath Wendy. She's nice and gentle."

"Me? Where?" said Ben. "In there? With them?" It was astonishing. It all happened so quickly he had no time to think. There he suddenly was, staring up at Wendy, with no barriers in between them.

Watching had been wonderful enough, but now the hosepipe was in Ben's hand. Wendy flipped back her trunk and opened her mouth.

Clare said, "Look, Ben's giving her a drink." His father was busy with the camera.

Ben sprayed and went on spraying, and he loved it and Wendy loved it. He moved to a back foot and touched it.

"Wendy, lift it," he said. Wendy looked round first, but then she did as he said. It was marvellous. He had ordered an elephant about on his birthday.

37

"Good girl," said Ben, washing under her foot. He did the other feet too, while the assistant scrubbed her with a brush that was too heavy for Ben.

Now Wendy played a trick on Ben. She slipped her trunk into his pocket and took out Clare's present. Wendy didn't know what a mouth organ was, but, as she breathed, *sounds* came out of it.

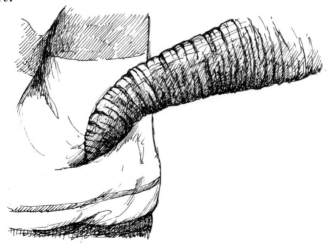

Everybody burst out laughing, Christina trumpeted, and Wendy dropped the strange thing into the keeper's hand.

He said, "Well, Ben. That wasn't planned."

Ben said, "They were singing 'Happy Birthday'. It's better than a party," said Ben, "better than anything."